CAPTAIN CAT

and the
Pirate Lunch

by Emma J. Virján

Ready-to-Read

Simon Spotlight
New York   London   Toronto   Sydney   New Delhi

For Elizabeth, my BFF

SIMON SPOTLIGHT
An imprint of Simon & Schuster Children's Publishing Division
1230 Avenue of the Americas, New York, New York 10020
This Simon Spotlight edition December 2021
Copyright © 2021 by Emma J. Virján
For information about special discounts for bulk purchases, please contact
Simon & Schuster Special Sales at 1-866-506-1949 or business@simonandschuster.com.
Manufactured in the United States of America 1121 LAK
10 9 8 7 6 5 4 3 2 1
ISBN 978-1-5344-9571-5 (hc)
ISBN 978-1-5344-9570-8 (pbk)
ISBN 978-1-5344-9572-2 (ebook)

Three yellow birds
land on a ship.

Three yellow birds
want to take a trip.

Three yellow birds
sit on a sail.

Two yellow birds
spot a blue whale.

Captain Cat hears
chirps from the deck.

Captain Cat goes
upstairs to check.

Captain Cat dreams about lunch.

Two yellow birds might be in a crunch.

Pour.  # Mix.

Sizzle.

Flip.

Melt.

Drizzle.

While Captain Cat
serves lunch and tea,

one yellow bird
flies out to sea.

One yellow bird seeks
help from the whale,

who comes to his aid
with a flap of its tail.

Whoosh.

Bam.

Splash.

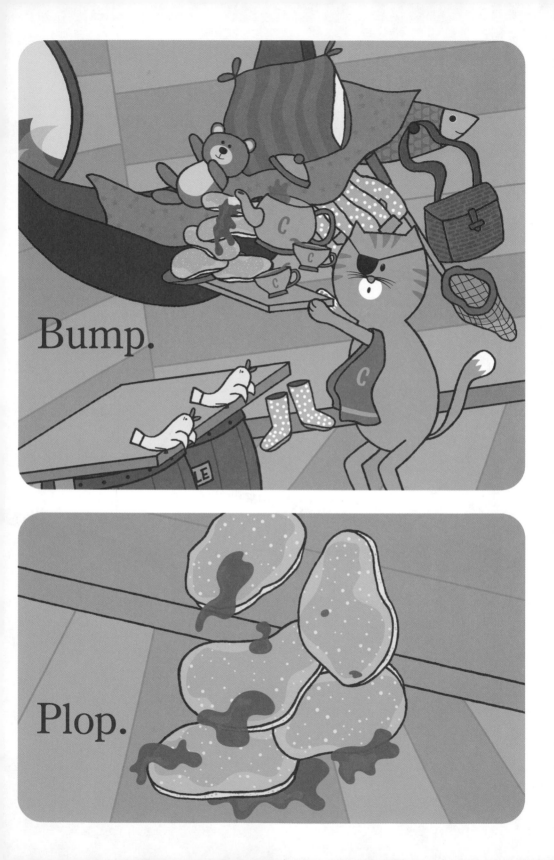

Crash.

One yellow bird stands by the door

and sees a mess
all over the floor.

We were having fun with Captain Cat.
I am sorry. I did not know that.

I get lonely when
out at sea.
I wanted some friends
to share lunch and tea.

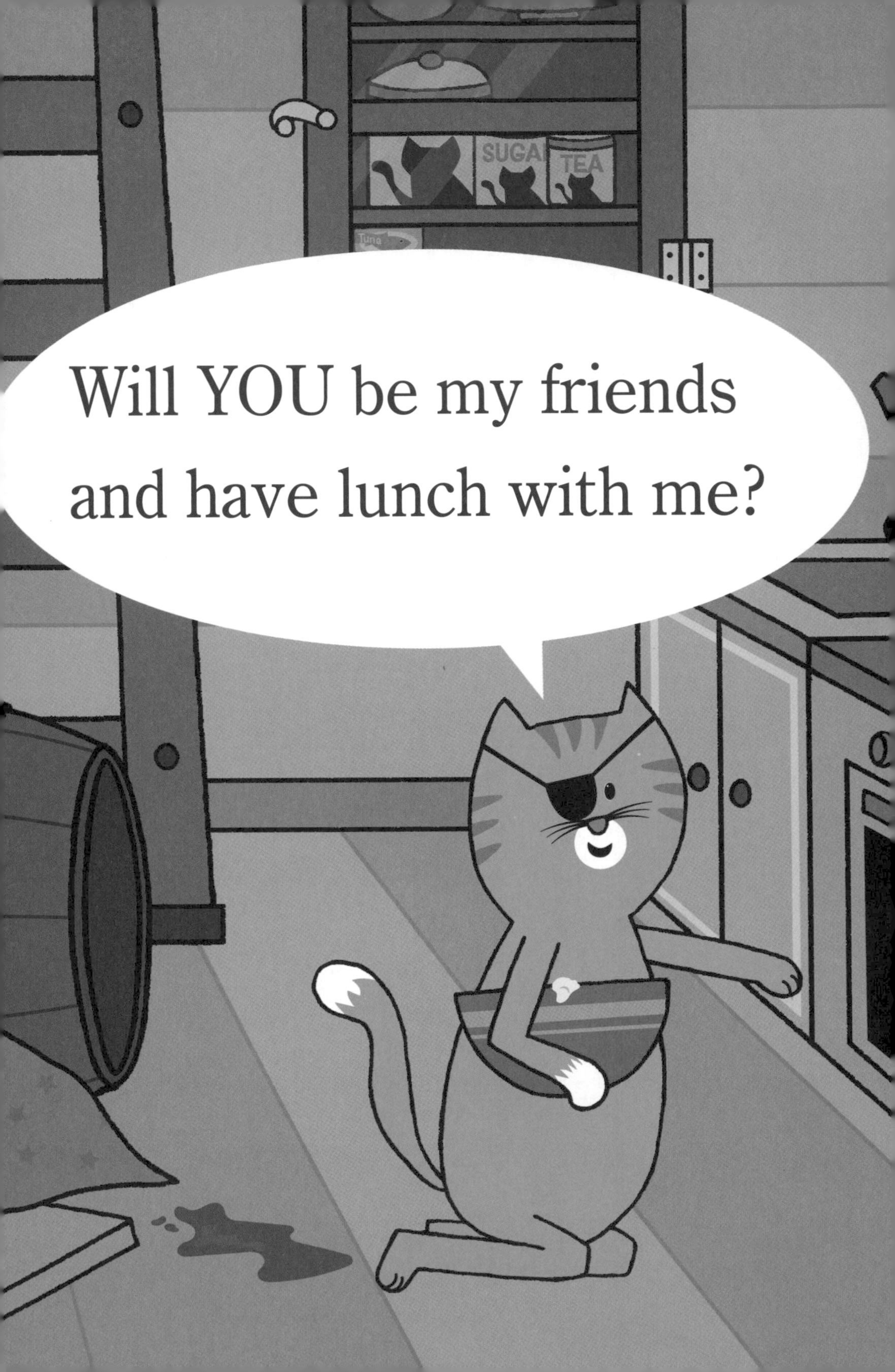
TEA
Will YOU be my friends and have lunch with me?

We agree!

We can make more lunch.

We can make more tea.

Four friends eat lunch under the sun

and ask the blue whale
to join in the fun.

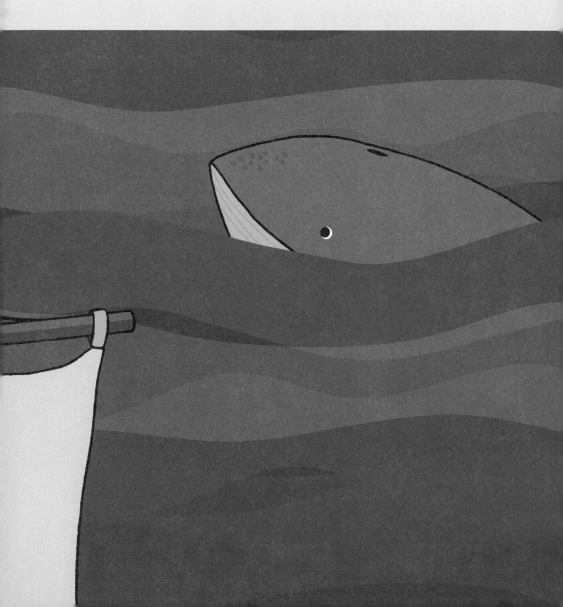

Then the five friends
take a trip!
One is in the ocean.
Four are on a ship.